D1252345

The Biggest, Meanest, Ugliest Dog in the Whole Wide World

By Rebecca C. Jones

Illustrated by Wendy Watson

Macmillan Publishing Company

New York

Macmillan Publishing Company
866 Third Avenue, New York, N.Y. 10022
Collier Macmillan Canada, Inc.
Printed in the United States of America

10 9 8 7 6 5 4

Library of Congress Cataloging in Publication Data
Jones, Rebecca C.
The biggest, meanest, ugliest dog in the whole wide world.
Summary: Jonathan is terrified of the dog next door, until
one day he throws his ball at it in defense
and their relationship changes.
[1. Dogs—Fiction] I. Watson, Wendy, ill. II. Title.
PZ7.J72478Bi [E] 82-6612 ISBN 0-02-747800-9 AACR2

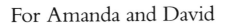

For Amanda and David

Jonathan lived next door to the biggest, meanest, ugliest dog in the whole wide world.

The dog had pointy black ears, sharp white teeth and a wicked crooked tail.

The dog belonged to Mr. and Mrs. McCreary. They called him Pirate. He had a sinister silver patch over one eye, and he was a thief. Once he got loose and stole Jonathan's new red boots off the front steps. He chewed on them until there was nothing left but the shiny black buckles.

Mrs. McCreary paid for the boots and said she was sorry. Jonathan was just glad he wasn't wearing the boots when Pirate decided to eat them.

Sometimes Pirate sat on his front
porch with his tongue hanging out.
Jonathan was sure he was looking
for little boys to eat.

Sometimes Pirate ran along the fence in his backyard and barked a loud and growly bark at Jonathan.

That's when Jonathan would run inside his house.

Sometimes Mrs. McCreary took Pirate for a walk. That's when Jonathan would cross the street.

And sometimes Mr. McCreary
took Pirate into his front yard to
play. That's when Jonathan would
climb a tree.

The big dog would stand at the bottom of the tree and bark his loud and growly bark at Jonathan. Jonathan could see the pointy black ears and the sharp white teeth and the wicked crooked tail.

Jonathan wouldn't come down until Pirate went home.

One day Jonathan was playing in his sandbox. He loaded a big pile of sand in his dump truck and moved it slowly down the main street of his sand city. It was a big, heavy truck and Jonathan made it say *vroom, vroom, var-room!*

The truck was so loud that Jonathan didn't hear someone come into his yard.

It was the biggest, meanest, ugliest dog in the whole wide world.

By the time Jonathan saw him, it was too late to run inside his house. There was no street to cross and no tree to climb.

Jonathan was alone with the biggest, meanest, ugliest dog in the whole wide world. He could see his pointy black ears and his sharp white teeth and his wicked crooked tail.

"Go away!" Jonathan shouted in his loudest voice. "Go away!"

The dog barked his loud and growly bark.

"Go away!" Jonathan shouted
again. He picked up his red ball and
threw it at the dog.

The dog chased the ball and brought it back to Jonathan. He dropped the ball at Jonathan's feet and sat down. He barked again, but this time it didn't sound so loud and growly.

Jonathan picked up the ball and
threw it again. The dog brought it
back.

Jonathan threw the ball again and again. Again and again Pirate brought it back.

After a while Pirate stopped chasing the ball. He sat in the grass and panted. Jonathan saw Pirate's tongue hanging out the way it did when he sat on his front porch.

Only this time Jonathan didn't think Pirate was looking for little boys to eat. He just thought Pirate looked very hot and tired.

Jonathan held out his hand. Pirate sniffed it. Then Pirate opened his mouth wide and took one big wet lick! It tickled.

Mrs. McCreary came running into Jonathan's yard.

"Oh, I'm sorry!" she cried. "I must have left the gate open and Pirate got out. I hope he didn't scare you."

"It's okay," Jonathan told her. "I'm not afraid of Pirate. Pirate and I are friends."

Jonathan knelt down and hugged the biggest, meanest, ugliest dog in the whole wide world.

Pirate wagged his wicked crooked tail—in a very friendly way.